The Early History of the Colonial Post-office

Mary Emma Woolley

Pharos Books

HB ISBN: 978-93-67002-17-9
ISBN: 978-93-67004-84-5
eISBN: 978-93-67009-66-6

Publisher: Pharos Books (P) Ltd.
Plot No.-63, 1st Floor, Main Mother Dairy Road
Pandav Nagar, East Delhi-110092
Phone: 011-40395855, +4049916623
WhatsApp: +91 9319228272
E-mail: bookspharos@gmail.com
Website: www.pharosbooks.in
Edition: 2025

Printed By: Sushma Book Binding House, Okhla Industrial Area, Phase II, New Delhi-110020

The Early History of the Colonial Post-Office
Mary Emma Woolley

CONTENTS

The Early History of the Colonial Post-Office

EARLY HISTORY OF THE COLONIAL POST OFFICE.

A letter written in 1652, by Samuel Symonds of Ipswich, to John Winthrop, Jr., at Pequot, says: "I cannot say but its besides my intentions that I write not more frequently unto you; I can onely plead this for my excuse (soe farr as it will goe) ... and the uncertainty when and how to convey letters."[1]

A glance at the correspondence of that period shows that Mr. Symonds was not the only one inconvenienced by the "uncertainty when and how to convey letters." With no domestic postal service the writers of that day were dependent upon individual bearers and pressed neighbors, relatives, merchants, sea captains, any and every one whom they could reach, into the service. Indians were often used as messengers. Roger Williams writing to John Winthrop, at some time in the '30's, speaks of word "by this bearer Wequash whome (being a Pequt himselfe) I commended for a guide in the Pequt expedition;" again, "I pray let your servant direct the native with this letter;" and at still another time, "From your owne hand (by Robin Causasenamont)."[2]

John Endicott writes to John Winthrop, April 13, 1638: "Your kinde lines I receaued by Mascanomet;" and a letter from the Isle of Wight (near Long Island), dated "Aprill 27, 1650," says, "I resavid yours by the Indian."[3]

Until 1639 there is no trace of a postal system, but under the *Massachusetts General Court Records*, of that year[4] (Nov. 5th), is the following entry: "For preventing the miscarriage of letters, ... It is ordered that notice bee given, that Richard Fairbanks, his house in Boston, is the place appointed for all letters, which are brought from beyond the Seas, or are to be sent thither; ... are to be brought unto him and he is to take care, that they bee delivered, or sent according to their directions and hee is alowed for every such letter 1*d.* and must answer all miscarriages through his owne neglect in this kind; provided that no man shall bee compelled to bring his letters thither except hee please."

This action on the part of the Massachusetts General Court was, as far as can be discovered, the first effort by the colonies to provide a post office. Eighteen years later, June 12, 1657, an ordinance was passed[5] by the director general and council of the New Netherlands, forbidding the boarding of incoming vessels until visited by the governing officer and the letters delivered, the penalty for evading the law being fixed at thirty guilders.[6]

Since private shippers were in the habit of taking letters from the New Netherlands and Curaçoa, without placing them in a sealed bag, the directors of the West India Company, at the chamber in Amsterdam, in 1659 (October 30) adopted a resolution requiring captains of vessels to enter into bond not to carry letters to Holland from New Netherlands or Curaçoa, unless received from persons authorized to collect them, under penalty of one hundred Carolus guilders; and on the second of the following June (1660) the director general and council of the colony passed an ordinance warning citizens to observe this resolution. A box was placed in New Amsterdam, in the office of the secretary of the province, for the receipt of letters, and for all those capable of registry, three stivers in wampum were to be paid. These movements on the part of Massachusetts and New Netherlands concerned foreign letters simply; until 1672 there were apparently no arrangements for the transmission and delivery of domestic letters. In December of that year, there was an effort to start a monthly post between New York and Boston, a project originating with Francis Lovelace, governor of New York. In a letter to John Winthrop, governor of Connecticut, dated December 27, 1672, he says:[7] "I herewith present you with 2 rarities, a pacquett of the latest intelligence I could meet withal, and a post ... by the latter you will meet with a monthly fresh supply; so that if it receive but the same ardent inclinations as first it hath from myself, by our monthly advisers all publique occurences may be transmitted between us, together with severall other great conveniencys of publique importance, consonant to the commands laid upon us by his sacred majestie, who strictly enjoins all his American subjects to enter into a close correspondency with each other ... this person that has undertaken the employment I conceaved most proper, being voted active, stout and indefatigable.... I have affixt an annuall sallery on him, which, together with the advantage of his letters and other small portable packes, may afford him a handsome livelyhood.... The maile has divers baggs, according to the towns the letters are designed to, which are all sealed up 'till their arrivement, with the seal of the secretarie's office, whose care it is on Saturday night to seale them up. Only by-letters are in an open bag, to dispense by the wayes.... I shall only beg of you your furtherance to so universall a good work; that is, to afford him directions where, and to whom to make his application to upon his arrival at Boston; as likewise to afford him what letters you can to establish him in that employment there. It would be much advantageous to our designe, if in the intervall you discoursed with some of the most able woodmen, to make out the best and most facile way for a post, which in processe of tyme would be the king's best highway; as likewise passages and accommodation at rivers, fords, or other necessary places."

The first post messenger started from New York, January 22, 1672/3, with sworn instructions to behave civilly, to inquire of Winthrop how to form the best post road, and to mark the trees for the direction of passengers.

To quote from the *Memorial History of New York*:[8] "It is recorded as creating great excitement in the little village of Harlem, when that first postman drew up at the tavern door to refresh himself, as he undoubtedly did, with some good home-brewed Harlem beer—his 'port mantles' (port manteaux) crammed with 'letters and small portable goods,' the 'locked box' in the office of the colonial secretary accumulating the next month's mail, and what he had brought, being carried to the 'coffee house' to be 'well thumbed' until called for." Notwithstanding this auspicious beginning, the project fell through, probably because of the Dutch and other wars of the time, and was not revived by this colony until 1684, when Thomas Dongan, governor of New York, and Thomas Treat, governor of Connecticut, conferred concerning a post between New York and the British colonies as far as Boston.[9]

In the meantime Massachusetts had taken up the question again,[10] the general court on January 6, 1673/4, ordering that post messengers, who had previously received no stated allowance, should thereafter receive 3*d.* a mile in money and full satisfaction for the expenses of man and beast.[11]

In 1677 (June 1), further action was taken, the general court, in response to a petition of sundry merchants of Boston,[12] appointing John Hayward, scrivener, to "take in and convey letters according to the direction;" evidently there was more than one candidate, and one account poetically says of the court's decision: "It Richard May suggested John Hayward selected." The same year (October 8, 1674), the general court of Connecticut, meeting at Hartford,[13] gave specific instructions regarding the allowance for post riders; from Rye to Hartford, 12*s.* for the expenses of the horse, and 20*s.* for those of the man, with the addition of 8*d.* from the "midle of October to the last of Aprill," and the special injunction that "hyred" horses should not be deprived of their allowance. The number of routes mentioned, twenty-four, shows the extent of the effort made at that time.

The next move came from New York, Gov. Dongan's proposition of 1684,[14] to which reference has already been made, adding to Lovelace's scheme of a post between New York and Boston, the suggestion that post houses be established along the coast from

Carolina to Nova Scotia. A letter to him from Sir John Werden (August 27, 1684), whose title to the profits from the English post office[15] was held to include the British provinces, approves the project and suggests that the privilege be offered for three or five years by way of form, with a reservation of not less than one-tenth of the profits to the duke. Six months later (February 18, 1684/5), Dongan writes[16] him that he had sent *permission* to set up a post house but no *power* to do it, although the neighboring colonies much desired it and in some places had established foot and horse messengers. He adds, "I am going to Connecticut to-morrow, to do all possible to settle a post office to Pemaquid this spring and endeavor settlement of post house at Boston."

On his return from Connecticut (March 2, 1684/5), the governor ordained in the New York council,[17] "That for the better correspondence between the colonies of America, a post office be established; and that the rates for riding post be per mile three pence; for every single letter, not above one hundred miles, three pence; if more, proportionably."

A letter[18] from Sir Edmund Andros to John Allyn, dated November 23, 1687, speaks of a contemplated post from Boston to the farthest settlements of Connecticut, John Perry to go between Hartford, Fairfield and Stamford once a month in the winter, and every three weeks during the summer, as Allyn suggests in his answer. A letter from Samuel Sewall[19] to Samuel Mather, at Windsor, Connecticut, as early as March 6, 1685/6[20], mentions John Perry as bearer and a postage of 3*d.* That this project was carried out is evident from the complaint brought before the council of New York[21] by John Perry, that on his way to Boston he was laid hold on by warrant from the usurper Leysler, brought to New York and his letters opened, the apparent object being to destroy commerce and trade.

June 11th, 1689, the Massachusetts general court[22] appointed Richard Wilkins, postmaster, to receive all letters and deliver them out at 1*d.* each.

In 1691/2, a new era opened for the colonial post office. On February 7th, of that year, William and Mary, by letters patent, granted[23] to "Thomas Neale, Esq., his executors, administrators and assignes, full power and authority to erect, settle and establish within the chief parts of their majesties' colonies and plantations in America, an office or offices for the receiving and dispatching letters and pacquets, and to receive, send and deliver the same under such rates and sums of money as the planters shall agree to give, and to hold and enjoy the same for the terme of twenty-one years."

To govern and manage the general post office,[24] Neale appointed (April 4th, 1692) Andrew Hamilton, an Edinburgh merchant, who in 1685 had emigrated to New Jersey, and become special agent of the proprietors.

On the deposition of Andros in 1689, Hamilton embarked for England to consult with the proprietors; on the voyage was taken prisoner by the French, but soon released, and in 1692 was made governor of New Jersey. Hamilton's application to the colonial legislatures[25] to "ascertain and establish such rates and terms as should tend to quicker maintenance of mutual correspondence among all neighboring colonies and plantations and that trade and commerce might be better preserved," met with a favorable response from the colonial governments.

He first presented the subject to Governor Fletcher and the New York legislature.[26] The council, meeting at Fort Wm. Henry, October 29, 1692,[27] after reading his proposition, and also a letter from the queen to the governor, urging him to assist Hamilton in settling the office, appointed Colonels Courtlandt and Bayard a committee[28] to deliver the proposition to the house of representatives, and in November (1692) the bill was passed by both houses and signed by the governor. The chief provisions of the bill are as follows:[29] A general letter office was to be "erected and established in some convenient place within the city of New York," one master of the general office to be appointed from time to time by Hamilton, who with his servant or agent should have the "receiving, taking up, ordering, dispatching, sending post or with speed and delivery of all letters and pacquets whatsoever, which shall from time to time be sent to and from all and every of the adjacent collonies and plantations on the main land and continent of America or any other of their majesties kingdoms and dominions beyond the Seas." The postmaster was to "prepare and provide horses and furniture unto all through posts and persons riding in post." Rates for single letters to or from Europe, the West Indies or elsewhere to and from beyond the seas, were 9*d.*, and the same from Boston or Maryland to New York; from Virginia, 12*d.*, and to or from any place not exceeding eighty miles from New York, four pence half penny.

All postmasters were freed from excise and all public services, with the exception of the postmaster of the city of New York, who was exempt only from public services. Any persons or "body politick or corporate others than the P. M. Gen. aforesaid" presuming to "carry, recarry or deliver letters for hire, other than as before excepted, or to set up or imploy any foot-post, horse-post or pacquet boat whatsoever" for the carrying of letters or pacquets, or providing "horses and furniture for the horses of any through posts, or persons riding post with a guide and horn," should forfeit £100 current money, one-half going to the governor and the other half to the postmaster-general. All letters and pacquets brought by ship or vessel were to be delivered to the postmaster of New York or to his servants, provided "that no letters going up or coming down Hudson's river and going to or from Long Island shall be carried to the post-office, everything herein contained to the contrary notwithstanding," this clause, together with that regarding exemption from public service and excise, being amendments by the council to the bill as presented by the house.

The act was in force for three years,[30] and in 1695 (July 2d and 3d) a bill was passed for continuing the act three years longer, "every article,[31] rule and clause therein mentioned to remain in full force and effect."

In 1699 (May 5) the act was again continued,[32] this time for two years, the new bill stating that "the advantage which the inhabitants of this province daily have, the mutual correspondence which they have with their neighboring collonies and plantations and for the promoting of trade and wealth of each other, encourage to the continuance of the same." In 1702[33] the act coming again before the Assembly and Council was continued for four and one-half years from 1700; and in 1705[34] (July 5, 6, 8 and 10, and August 14) it was re-continued for three years from October, 1704.[35]

Concerning the passage of this act Lord Cornbury wrote to the Lords of Trade that it was absolutely necessary; otherwise the post to Boston and Philadelphia would be lost.[36]

At the meeting[37] of the first session of the eleventh Assembly at Fort Anne, August 20, 1708, Governor Cornbury in his opening speech said:[38] "I can't omit putting you in mind that Act for encouraging a Post Office is expired; that it is of so general Advantage that I hope you will revive it." The next month (September 3, 7, 10, 13, and 18, 1708) the act was considered and passed. At a meeting of the council in New York,[39] June 21, 1709, one of the members was ordered to go to the assembly and "desire them to provide for and settle a Post from Albany to Westfield for holding a Correspondence Between Boston and Albany for the service of the present Expedition the Province of Massachusetts Bay having already settled a Post from Boston to Westfield;" but action was not taken before 1715.

The letters of this period throw light upon the condition of the post with regard to regularity and frequency.

The Earl of Bellomont writing from New York[40] to Secretary Popple in London, May 25, 1698, says: "The sure way of conveying letters to me is by way of Boston, whence the post comes every week to this place;" and Lord Cornbury writes to the Lords of Trade,[41] December 12, 1702: "But I entreat your Lordspps to consider that but few ships goe directly from this port to England, So that I must depend upon the Boston and Philadelphia posts for conveying my letters to such ships as may be going to England; and sometimes both these Conveyances faile;" and again in a letter to the Lords of Trade, June 30, 1704:[42] "I beg your Lordspps to consider likewise the difficulty I lye under, with respect to opportunity's of writing into England, which is thus—The post that goes through this place goes Eastward as far as Boston, but Westward he goes no further than Philadelphia and there is no other post upon all this Continent, so that I have any letters to send to Virginia or to Maryland I must either send an Express who is often retarded for want of boats to cross those great rivers they must go over or else for want of horses, or else I must send them by some passengers who are going thither. The least I have known any Express take to go from hence to Virginia, has been three weeks, so that very often, before I can hear from Coll: Nicholson what time the fleet will sail and send my packets, the fleet is sailed. I hope we shall find a way to remedy that shortly, for Coll: Nicholson and Coll: Seymour have wrote me word that they will be here in September, and I do then intend to propose to them the settling of a Post, to go through to Virginia.... I must further acquaint Your Lordspps that our letters do not come safe by the way of Boston, I have had several letters by that way which have been broken open."

Cornbury's scheme, as he tells us in another letter to the Lords of Trade, written November 6, 1704,[43] was to lay a tax in each province by act of assembly, for defraying the charges of the post, which might then have gone from Boston to North Carolina, but his failure to meet the men with whom he proposed to discuss it, thwarted the plan.

June 9, 1693, Massachusetts passed in council[44] an act for encouraging the post office, selecting Boston as the place for the general letter office, the master to be appointed by Hamilton. Rates to Europe or to any place beyond the seas, were fixed at 2*d.*, to different places within the colonies, they varied according to distance; from Boston to Rhode Island they were 6*d.*, to the Connecticut colonies 9*d.*, to New York 12*d.*, to Eastern Pennsylvania or to Western Jersey 15*d.*, and to Maryland or to Virginia 2*s.* A fine of 40*s.* in the current money of the colony, was imposed upon those who carried or delivered letters without authority, one-half the fine recurring to their majesties for the support of the government of the province, and one-half to the postmaster-general for suing and prosecuting for same. Non-delivery or neglect of maintaining a constant post was fined 5*s.*, one-half going to their majesties and one-half to the party aggrieved; the ferryman "neglecting, refusing or delaying conveyance," also forfeited 5*s.* The postmaster was to pay the shipmaster one-half penny for each letter or pacquet brought, but all letters of public concern for their majesties' service were to be free of charge.

That the first few years of the post in Massachusetts were not very lucrative, is shown by the numerous complaints of grievances and petitions of Duncan Campbell, appointed by Hamilton deputy postmaster.[45] The charges are thrice the income, he complains, and begs that a salary be given, urging the example of the governor and assembly of New York in voting £50 per annum for the support of the office in that province. This petition meeting with no response, he asked for freedom from public rates, taxes and excise for retailing strong drink, and in 1694 (June 20) obtained a grant of £25 per annum from the public treasury of the province for two years. In 1696 (May 27) he petitioned for a renewal of the act encouraging a post office and also for a continuation of the postmaster's salary. The salary was voted (July 1, 1696), but no steps taken toward reviving the Post Office Act, for in 1703 (May 26) John Campbell[46] renewed the petition to the general court stating that the act had not been in force after 1696, and praying that since Hamilton was out of purse to the extent of £1,400 restitution might be made by a continuance of the privilege to his heirs.[47] The same petition was presented to Governor Joseph Dudley and to the council and representatives in General Assembly two months later (June 3, 1703), but with no result as far as renewal was concerned. Five years later (Nov. 3, 1708), a committee was appointed to inquire what allowance should be made for encouraging the post office, but up to the time of Queen Anne's Act in 1710 no decision had been reached.

Campbell's memorandum of 1703 (July 19) is interesting as showing the cost of maintaining the office between Philadelphia and Piscataqua. The annual outlay was £680, and the receipts little more than £400, leaving a deficit of £275.

The Campbells had other grievances.[48] In a petition to the governor, the council and the assembly, soon after the act of 1693, Duncan begged that a fine be imposed for failure to deliver letters from ships to the postmaster. In 1694 the request was repeated, and in answer to this petition a bill was presented ordering all persons not bringing letters which ought to be delivered into the post office, to pay four times as much as was due on the letters, damages to be made good to the party injured. The house voted in the affirmative May 8, 1694/5, but the council seems to have taken no action in the matter. In 1696 (May 27) Campbell sent a similar petition, asking also that the rates on foreign letters might be advanced from two to three pence, and the payment to masters of ships from an half penny to 1*d.*, "which," he adds, "will be a great encouragement to masters not to deliver news to other persons."

In 1703, John Campbell offered a memorial to the general court, complaining "that every body carrying of letters to and from towns where post offices are settled, is a very great hindrance and discouragement to said office," letters from Connecticut colony being carried to Piscataqua, and after lying in the office there some weeks and months, at last come to Boston, the office being blamed for the delay without a cause, and that one-half the letters from Europe and West Indies and other places by sea, were not brought to the office at all. The ferrymen also came in for their share of blame, as being very backward in carrying those employed in the post office, sometimes even demanding money for ferriage. The petition was granted (July 22, 1703), and £20 for the year past and £40 for the one ensuing allowed to Campbell. Again in 1706 (April 12 and October 30) £50 was granted to him. In 1709 (November 18) he wrote to the Governor that six months after his appointment by Hamilton in 1701, he had represented to the General Assembly that he could not serve, since the salary was so small, and two members of the upper house had then suggested a salary of £40, which, reduced by the vote of the lower house to £20, had been paid until within three years. He recalled the fact that the post office saved the country above £150 per annum, which it would be obliged to pay for express, if there were no office. The public letters, passed free, had cost more than the postmaster's allowance, besides the charge of sending the governor's letters weekly to Roxbury "in times of snow or rain." The queen, unwilling to augment the charge of the office to what it was in Hamilton's time, was then at above £200 sterling charges yearly, to support it between New Hampshire and Pennsylvania, and if the several offices had half salary allowed them, it would cost her majesty £100 sterling more. Accordingly he thought it but just that public letters for the time past should be paid for, the postmaster recompensed for sending the governor's letters to Roxbury, and some provision made for conveying them in the future. Otherwise, he would be obliged to represent the case to the postmaster-general of Great Britain, which he had foreborne to do, hoping that the general court would prevent it.

The council took no cognizance of the petition, as we learn from its renewal in 1711.[49]

The action of New Hampshire relative to a post, occurred at about the same time as that of Massachusetts. John Usher,[50] writing to the New Hampshire council, from Boston, March 25, 1693, said that the postmaster-general in Boston was desirous of knowing what salary would be allowed or how much a letter for a post from Piscataqua to Boston, adding that it might be an advantage to gain news from England and the West Indies, and that they would like a post weekly or once in two weeks. The council (March 27, 1693) was of the opinion[51] that a post was necessary, and that there should be an allowance per letter, according to other places in like circumstances, proportionate to the distance from Boston, "Every one to pay for his own Lett^{r}." A record[52] in the "Journal of the Council and Assembly" of July 29, 1693, says: "Maj. Vaughan and Mr. Waldron were appointed to prepare and drawe up a Bill for settling a Post Office in this Province," and on the fourth of August the council concurred with the bill which had been passed by the lower house.

It was enacted that[53] "a Poste Office and officers be henceforth appointed and settled in some Convenient place within the Towne of Portsmouth for Receiveing & dispatching awaye according to direction all letters and packetts that shall be brought thereinto & no Person or Persons whatsoever shall presume to Carry or recarry any letter or letters for hire but only such as belongs to the Poste Office dureing their power and authority from the aforesaid Thos. Nele Except such letters of Merchants and Masters which shall be sent by any Master of any Ship Boat or other vessel of Merchandise or by any other Person employed by them for the carrying of such letters aforesaid According to the Respective Direction And also Except letters to be sent by any private friend or friends in their way of Journey or Travill or by any Messenger or Messengers sent on purpose for or concerning the private affaires of any Person or Persons." Whoever offended against this Act should "forfeit the sum of ten pounds one halfe to their Majesties Towards the support of the Governor of this province The other halfe to the Postmaster Genrl." All "Letters & Packetts" were to be delivered by the importer at the post house or to the post officer, receiving in return a half-penny for each, the person to whom directed paying two pence for each letter, and for a "Packett no lesse than 3 letters besides Bills Loading Invoyces Gazette etc four pence. And for each letter brought from Boston in to this Province not exceeding five pence and Doble for a Packett and so proportionately for Letters on this sid Boston shall be paid with the customary allowance in the Government from whense they come." Neglect of duty in keeping constant post or in delivering letters was punishable by a fine of £5, "The one halfe to their Majesties the other halfe to the party agreved." All letters concerning their majesties' service were to be received and dispatched with all possible speed free from charge. It was "further enacted and ordained that the officer of the Post House haveing Licence granted to Retaile Beer Sider & Ale within Doors according to Law shall have his Excise free and no officer of the Excise shall demand anything of him for the same and his Person to be excused from watching and warding." The foregoing Act was to continue in force for three years from the publication, but in 1694 (May 12th), an additional act for the encouragement of the post office was passed,[54] since "notwithstanding a late act for the Setling a Poste Office within this Province Sundrie Letters are brought by ships and other vessell a longe shore to the Prejudice of those who are at the charge of keeping a poste goeing once a week by land." It was "Enacted by the Liet. Governor Counsill & Representatives convened in Genl. Assembly" that thereafter all masters of sloops or other vessels arriving within the Province should deliver all letters brought in by them, except such as concerned the loading of their vessels, to the collector or other post officer to be carried "with all convenient speed" to the post house.

The next year (May 21, 1695), a petition from Campbell for encouraging the post office, was answered by a bill settling a salary of £12 for the ensuing year.[55] In 1698[56] (April 7th) another petition from Campbell for continuing the support of the post office was read in the council and sent to the assembly, but returned without their allowing anything. July 2d, 1703, a committee of both houses was appointed to consider the petition of John Campbell, Duncan's successor, and in February (8th), 1703/4, £21 4*s.* was voted.

A year later[57] (May 3d, 1705) the council and General Assembly voted to pay £6 out of the next provincial rate, to Campbell for his "extraordinary Service in forwarding his Excellency's and Government letters for her Majesty's service relating to this province;" again in 1707 (April 8th) he was granted[58] £6 out of the treasury, and in 1708 (May 6th) another £6 for "diligent care of expresses and letters."

The first entry in the Colonial Records of Rhode Island[59] regarding a post is in 1774.

Connecticut's earliest efforts toward the establishment of a post have already been mentioned in connection with New York and Massachusetts. On May 10th, 1694, the court of election at Hartford passed the following Act for the encouragement of a post office.[60]

"Whereas their most excelent Maties King Wm and Queen Mary by their letters pattents have granted a Post Office to be set up in these partes of N. E. for the receiving and disspatching of letters and pacquetts from one place to another for their Maties speciall service and the benefit of theire Maties good Subjects in these parts. This court being willing to encourage so good a worke, doe order and enact that all such persons as shall be imployed by the Post Master Gen. in the severall stages within this Colony of Connecticut shall and may pass and repasse all and every ferry within this Colony, from the day of the date hereof for and during this courts pleasure, without payeing any rate or sume of money either for his own or horses passage."

May, 1698,[61] in response to a complaint that posts and other travellers met with great difficulty in journeying through the colony, especially in the township of Stonington, the court ordered the selectmen to lay out convenient highways, kept cleared and open, unless they passed through ancient common fields, or the general or county court ordered otherwise, and "made good with sufficient causeis and bridges as need shall require," failure to observe these instructions to be punished by a fine of £10 into the public treasury, and for a continuance of the offence by an annual fine of £10 to be levied upon the selectment or inhabitants.

In May, 1704,[62] the general court decreed that since the post was often impeded, "in cases extraordinarie the authoritie may grant a bill to the Constables for the defraying of such charges as are really necessary."

Watson,[63] in his *Annals of Philadelphia*, bases on MSS. in the possession of the Pemberton family, his statement that as early as July, 1683, a weekly post was established by order of William Penn and a grant given to a certain Henry Waldy of Tekonay to hold one, and "supply passengers with horses from Philadelphia to New Castle or the Falls of the Delaware; the rates from the Falls to Philadelphia 3*d.*, to Chester 5*d.*, to New Castle 7*d.*, to Maryland 9*d.*, and from Philadelphia to Chester 2*d.*, to New Castle 4*d.*, to Maryland 6*d.*." Winsor, in the *Narrative and Critical History*, adds that the notices of the departure of the post were put on the meeting-house doors and in other public places.

The same year (1683)[64] a law was passed at Philadelphia directing the way in which official letters should be dispatched, in order that the governor might obtain "true and speedy information regarding public affairs, as well from Europe as the neighboring colonies and remote parts of this province and territories thereof." "Be it Enacted by the authority aforesaid, That every Justice of the Peace, Sheriff or Constable within the respective counties of this province and territories thereof, to whose hands or knowledge any Letter or Letters shall come, directed to or from the governor, shall dispatch them, within 3 hours at the farthest, after the receipt or knowledge thereof, to the next Sheriff or Constable, and so forwards, as the Letter directs, upon the penalty of 20*s.* for every hour's delay. And in such cases, all Justices of the Peace, Sheriffs or Constables are hereby empowered to press either man or horse for that service, allowing for a horse or man, 2 pence by the mile, to be paid out of the public stock."

September 5th, 1700, Penn writes to Logan that he sends a package for Governor Blackeston[65] to be forwarded to the sheriff of New Castle, showing that the custom was in vogue seventeen years after its origin.

The *Duke of Yorke's Laws*[66] under the laws made and passed by Benjamin Fletcher, governor of Pennsylvania, and the council and representatives, May 15th and June 1st, 1693, records one for the erection of a post office in Philadelphia by Andrew Hamilton, "from whence all letters & packets may be with all expedition sent into any of the parts of New England and other adjacent colonies in these parts of America, at which said office all returns and answers may be received." Andrew Hamilton, or some other postmaster-general appointed by the king, was to demand and receive postage according to the following rates: single foreign letters 2*d.*, and each packet 4*d.*; letters sent from Philadelphia to New York 4*d.* half penny, to Connecticut 9*d.*, to Rhode Island 12*d.*, to Boston 15*d.*, to points beyond Boston 19*d.*, to Maryland and Virginia 9*d.*, and to every place within eighty miles of Philadelphia 4*d.* half penny. If foreign letters were left forty-eight hours uncalled for, they were to be delivered and one penny more for each demanded from receiver. Public letters were to go post free; ferriage was to be free for all, and constant posts were to be maintained from Philadelphia to New York and New Castle.

At an assembly held at Philadelphia,[67] May 20th, 1697, Joseph Growden, "chairman of the grand comittee appointed to consider of Andrew Hamilton's memorial for encouragement to support the post," reported "that it was the vote of the comittee that a bill be prepared for encouragement to support the post both by the publick and upon private letters."

Since the charge of the office had much exceeded the postage,[68] the assembly, "being sensible of the benefit of the said office to trade and commerce, and to the province and territories in general if it be continued, and of the great loss that will happen to both if it should happen to fall for want of encouragement," it was voted that the rates be raised on foreign letters received from 2*d.* to 4*d.*, on those sent from Philadelphia to New York from 4½*d.* to 8*d.*, and other rates proportionately. Hamilton was to receive £20 in the silver money of the province from the public treasury annually for three years, the period during which the law was to be in force.

In 1700, a bill was passed to be in effect seven years, which says:[69]

"Considering that maintenance of speedy correspondence is good for trade and is best carried on by public post, Be it enacted, that there be a General Letter Office erected and established in Philadelphia to send letters to colonies planted in America or in any of the King's Kingdoms in foreign lands." Rates were regulated by bulk, as well as by distance, a sheet of paper being accounted as a single letter and a packet equal to three letters, at the least; the post of a single letter from Philadelphia to Boston or Rhode Island was 18*d.*, to Piscataqua and other parts east of Boston 2*s.*, to New York 8*d.*, to Maryland and Virginia 18*d.* if by post, if by private person to the office 4*d.*, all letters for the proprietary or for the governor to be free. The fine for a neglectful ferryman was £5, for any one who should presume to carry letters for hire or set up or employ any post, £40.

"Whereas, letters to merchants were often delayed and given to untrustworthy persons who may open them and get trade secrets," shipmasters were ordered to give letters only to the postmaster or to his assistants.

In 1701 (June 23d), in response to a petition from Patrick Robinson in behalf of Col. Andrew Hamilton, "Postmaster General in America and Gov[r] of the Jerseys," praying for the payment from the "publick stock" of the £20 per year for three years, which had been allowed him by the act of 1697, the treasurer was ordered to pay the sum as soon as there was sufficient money in his hands.

April 11th, 1706,[70] a grant was given a certain Hugh Huddy to establish stages from Burlington to Perth Amboy, and April 4th, 1709, an act for the encouragement of the post office was passed by the New Jersey assembly. The masters of the offices were to be appointed from time to time by the postmaster-general. No other persons were to receive, dispatch or deliver letters or packets except such as were sent by masters or merchants in ships of which, or of the cargo of which, they were entirely or in part owners, or "except letters to be sent by any private Friend or Friends in their ways of journey or Travel, or by any Messenger or Messengers sent of purpose for or concerning the private affairs of any person or persons."[71] The rates were fixed according to bulk as well as distance, the post of every single letter from Europe, the West Indies and other parts beyond the seas, was four pence half-penny, all letters to be accounted single if they did not exceed one sheet of paper. The postage on each "pacquet" of letters from these places was 9*d.* a "pacquet" being accounted three sheets, at the least. The post of every letter from Boston not exceeding one sheet of paper, was 1*s.* 3*d.*, the post of every letter not exceeding two sheets, 2*s.* 6*d.*, and the post of every "pacquet of letters or other things whatsoever, 2*s.* 6*d.* for every ounce, Troy weight, and for the post of every letter not exceeding one sheet of paper, for any place not exceeding one hundred and fifty miles, 9*d.*, and so in proportion to the bulk." Carrying letters for hire, or setting up or employing any foot, post, horse or paquet boat for carrying letters or paquets or providing and maintaining horses or furniture for the horsing of any through post, was punishable by a fine of £100 current money for every several offence, one-third to go to the governor, one-third to the use of the colony and the remaining third to the informer. Any ferryman neglecting, delaying or refusing to convey posts forfeited £5.

As late as 1791 there were only six post offices in the colony, and none south of Trenton.[72]

The Maryland archives contain no reference to a post before 1710.

In March, 1661/2, the following act[73] was passed by the Virginia assembly: "Whereas the remotenesse of diverse places in the country from James Citty and the necessity of communicating diverse businesses to the utmost lymitts of itt, would (if messengers were purposely prest) put the country to an annuall greate expense for prevention whereof, Be it enacted that all letters superscribed for the service of his Majesty or publique shall be imediately conveyed from plantation to plantation to the place and person they are directed to under the penalty of 350 pounds of tobacco to each defaulter."

March 2d, 1692/3,[74] an act was passed for encouraging the erection of a post office in each county of the colony, Thomas Neale and his deputies to settle and establish the post at their own cost. Rates were to vary according to bulk and distance, state letters and public orders of the governor and council were to be sent free, and merchants were not to be prohibited from sending letters by the masters of vessels or others. The act was to be in force during the term granted by their majesties' letters patent to Thomas Neale.

Cooper's *Statutes at Large of South Carolina*[75] records an enactment regarding the post, of September 10th, 1702, by John Grenville, Esq., Pallatine, and the other lords and proprietors of the province of Carolina with the consent of the other members of the General Assembly. A certain Ed. Bourne was appointed postmaster and ordered to fix an exact list of letters received and dispatched in some public place in his house for thirty days, for each packet or letter receiving one-half royal, and for any neglect of duty forfeiting 40*s*. July 12th, 1707, an act[76] to erect a general post office was ratified and continued for two years.

The first act regarding a post office in North Carolina was in 1787.[77]

The correspondence of the period shows when the post became an established fact. About 1700, letters begin not with the names of the bearers, but with expressions such as the following: "The post is just blowing his horn and cannot help it that I write no more particularly."[78] "I had not time to say more by the last post than I did." "Sent by post last week." "Having no letter from you by the post." Individual bearers were still made use of, often probably for the reason which Logan gives in a letter to Penn, written February, 1708.[79] "I send this chiefly to accompany the enclosed to Wm. Aubrey, I therefore request thee to peruse it ... and to let it be sealed up, directed in some hand like mine, as J. Jeffreys, and delivered. I send it thus without cover to save postage, which is now very high to Boston." It is to be hoped that Lovelace's description of the first post as "active, stout and indefatigable," would apply equally to his successors, for they too went laden with "letters, portable goods and divers bags." Wait Winthrop writes from Boston to Fitz-John Winthrop, "Govr of his Maj^{ts} Collonye of Conecticott in New London," "I have had yours by the post with little bundle;" "If Sudance can bundle up John's freise Jacket & Mingoe's cloth Jacket in an old towell pray let the post bring them." "Post will bring you a pair of Simpsons ... could not goe to direct the man about the glass, or els it had gone by this Post" and "If Anthony has lamed the horses he may dispatch them quite that they may be no further trouble; but if their legs are fit to bring them, I desire they may be sent by the post, unless some safer opportunity present in two or three days."[80]

The early history of the colonial post office ends in 1710. With Queen Anne's Act of that year a new era began, introducing a system of greater uniformity, of greater detail and of closer connection with the home government.

MARY E. WOOLLEY.

PATENT TO THOMAS NEALE.

[The preceding pages were reprinted from the Publications of the Rhode Island Historical Society, January, 1894. Subsequently there was received from the Public Record Office in London, by the kindness of Hubert Hall, Esq., F.S.A., a copy of the patent to Thomas Neale, mentioned on page 8, preceding. The document is of fundamental importance to the history of the colonial post office. It instituted, for the first time, a royal intercolonial post, an American post office; and the American post office was the first of American executive departments, the first continental institution, and contributed, in its way, toward the unification of America. The patent is therefore given in full below. It is believed that it has never before been printed. It is designated, "Patent Roll (Chancery) 4 William and Mary, Part I, No. 3." Its date proves to be February 17, 1691/2, not February 7.

The patent to Thomas Neale was a piece of court favor. A few facts respecting the man himself may be of interest. Thomas Neale was an amusing person. All that the editor has been able to discover respecting him shows, with the utmost consistency, the confirmed office-holder, the determined and adventurous speculator, quick to seize any opportunity for personal profit. In the first place, as to his marriage. Pepys, January 1, 1663/4, mentions that there was much talk at the coffee-house about a very rich widow, said to be worth £80,000, and young and handsome. Her husband, Sir Nicholas Gold, a merchant, had not been dead a week yet, and already great courtiers were looking after her. She was the daughter of Sir John Garrard (Burke, Extinct and Dormant Baronetage, 214). June 20, 1664, Pepys tells a remarkable story of the bold manner in which Neale had won this prize, Lady Gold and he having been married in spite of her brother's opposition. By 1684 Neale had become installed in the palace, in the doubtless lucrative office of groom porter (*London Gazette*, July 28, 1684; Malcolm, "Anecdotes of London down to 1700," i. 378, iii. 50). The duties of this office are described by Pepys under date of January 1, 1667/8. "They were," says Macaulay (iv. 391), "to call the odds when the Court played at hazard, to provide cards and dice, and to decide any dispute which might arise on the bowling-green or at the gaming table." Neale organized lotteries after the Venetian manner, and in 1694 built extensively, for speculative purposes, about the Seven Dials (Evelyn's Diary, Nov. 14, 1693; Oct. 5, Nov. 22, 1694). In that same year he was employed by the government to conduct the lottery loan for the State, though some, says Macaulay, thought the treasury lowered itself thereby. But, after all, he was more of a personage than would, perhaps, be gathered from Macaulay's description. If he was not identical with the Thomas Neale who represented Petersfield in the Parliament of 1661-78 (Parl. Hist., iv. 198), he was certainly member for Ludgershall in all the subsequent parliaments of Charles II., in that of James II., and in the second and third parliaments of King William (5 W. & M., c. 7, sec. 69; letter of F. Bonnet to the Elector of Brandenburg, in Ranke, vi. 238; Parl. Hist., iv. 1082, 1157, 1301, 1346, v. 544, 961; Grey's Debates, viii. 380). Moreover, a list in Harl. Misc. viii. 512, prepared in July, 1698, identifies him with Thomas Neale, the master of the mint, Sir Isaac Newton's predecessor in that office. No doubt he was the author of a pamphlet on "Mending the Coin," London: 1695, which Allibone mentions. In fact, Neale was master of the mint from 1679 to 1699 (Ruding, Annals of the Coinage, i. 29, 35, ii. 30, 33, 46, 466). As the office was for life, and Newton succeeded upon a vacancy (Brewster's Sir Isaac Newton, ii. 193), it is probable that Neale died in 1699. He should have died rich, for a report in the Commons' Journals in 1697 (xi. 447, 453) gives us the characteristic touch that by his percentages on coinage he made apparently above £14,000 a year, while a deputy, paid

£400, did almost all the work in his absence. Yet it seems that he died insolvent, and failed to carry out a large building contract into which he had entered with Sir Walter Clarges (Malcolm, Londin. Rediv., iv. 328). Malcolm also says (Anecdotes of London in the Eighteenth Century, i. 36) that he left money for a charity school. The "Gentleman's Magazine" (ii. 631), mentions, under date of Feb. 17, 1732, the death of the widow of Thomas Neale, Esq., act. 96, in Old Palace Yard.

By way of corrigendum to Miss Woolley's paper, it should be mentioned, out of Mr. F. H. Norton's notes to his edition of the Journal of Hugh Finlay, that the Virginian act of 1661/2, cited on p. 22, above, was preceded by an act of similar tenor in 1657.—EDITOR.]

D coñ

Neale Ar?

Grant

3

WILLIAM AND MARY by the Grace of God &c To all to whome these presents shall come GREETING whereas our Trusty and welbeloved servant Thomas Neale Esquire hath lately humbly represented unto us that there never yet hath bin any post established for the conveying of Letters within or between Virginia Maryland Delaware New Yorke New England East and West Jersey Pensilvania and Northward as far as our Dominions reach in America And that the want thereof hath bin a great hindrance to the Trade of those parts And he the said Thomas Neale haveing humbly desired us to grant to him Letters Patents for the settling of such a post at his owne charge and Wee being fully satisfied that the same may be of service to Trade and correspondence and alsoe willing to encourage such an undertakeing know yee therefore that wee of our especiall grace certaine knowledge and meer moc?on and with and under the condic?ons and agreements herein after mentioned on the part and behalfe of the said Thomas Neale his executors and assignes to be performed have given and granted and by these presents for us our heires and successors doe give and grant unto the said Thomas Neale his executors administrators and assignes full power and authority to erect settle and establish and from time to time dureing the Terme herein after mentioned shall and may continue and enjoy within every or any the chiefe Ports of the severall Iselands Plantac?ons or Colonies belonging or to belong unto us our heires or successors in America an Office or Offices for the receiving and dispatching away of letters and packquetts with full power and authority and free liberty leave and lycence to and for him the said Thomas Neale his executors administrators and assignes and to and for such person or persons as he or they shall from time to time in this behalfe nominate to receive at the respective Offices aforesaid of and from any Masters of Ships Passengers or others any letters or Pacquetts whatsoever which shall be brought into the said Colonyes and Iselands or any of them from England or from any other parts whatsoever or which shall be sent from any parts or places of such respective Colony or Iseland to any other parts or places of the same and to dispatch send away carry and deliver the same to the respective persons and places to whome or which they shall be directed or sent within the said Colonys and Iselands or any of them and to take or receive to the onely use and behoofe of him the said Thomas Neale his executors administrators and assignes for the postage or conveyance of all such letters and Packquetts as shall be soe dispatcht sent away carried and delivered such rates and sumes of money as shall be proportionable to the rates for the post or carriage of letters sett downe and ascertained in and by an Act of Parliament made in the Twelfth yeare of the reigne of our late Royall Uncle King Charles the Second of Blessed memory entituled (an act for erecting and establishing a Post Office) or such other rates or sum?es of money as the Planters and others will freely agree to give for their letters or Pacquetts upon the first settlement of such Office or Offices And further Wee have given and granted and by these presents for us our heires and successors doe give and grant unto the said Thomas Neale his executors administrators and assignes and to such person and persons as he or they shall from time to time nominate as aforesaid full power and authority and free liberty leave and lycence at the said Office or offices so to be settled as aforesaid to collect and receive such letters or pacquetts as the Planters or any others will send or bring to the same and to dispatch such of them away for England as shall be directed thither by the first ship that from time to time shall be bound for any Port Towne of England to be there delivered to the Deputy or Deputies of our Postmaster or Postmasters Generall for the time being by him or them appointed or to be appointed for the said Port Towne To the end such Deputy or Deputys may from time to time send the same away to the Generall Post Office in England to be delivered according to the severall and respective direc?c?ons of the same as by the said Act of Parliament is prescribed and to dispatch away such of the said letters or Pacquetts as shall be directed or are to be carried from any of the said Islands Colonys or Plantac?ons from time to time To have hold use exercise and enjoy the said Office and Offices with the powers authorities priviledges leave and lycence herein before mentioned and intended to be hereby granted and to take perceive and receive the rates and sumes aforesaid unto him the said Thomas Neale his executors administrators and assignes To the onely use and behoofe of him the said Thomas Neale his executors administrators and assignes from the date of these our Letters Patents for and dureing the Terme of twenty one yeares from thence next ensueing and fully to be compleate and ended without any account or other matter or thing to be therefore rendered or paid to us our heires or successors other then the rent covenants and agreements herein after mentioned rendring to us our heires and successors dureing the said Terme the yearly rent of six shillings and eight pence to be paid into our Exchequer in England at the Feast of St. Michaell the Archangell yearly And Wee doe hereby for us our heirs and successors authorize and com?and the Postmaster and Postmasters Generall now and for the time being of us our heires and successors from time to time to issue such Deputac?ons as may better enable the said Thom Thomas Neale his executors administrators and assignes and such person or persons as he or they shall from time to time nominate to exercise and execute the powers and authorities to him or them hereby given and granted or menc?oned or intended to be given and granted in and about the premisses dureing the said Terme of Twenty one yeares and Wee doe hereby also for us our heires and successors strictly prohibit and forbid all and every person and persons whatsoever (other then the said Thomas Neale his executors administrators and assignes and such person or persons as he or they shall nominate as aforesaid) to sett up exercise or execute the like Office or Offices within the Iselands Colonys and Plantations aforesaid or any of them at any time or times within or during the continuance of the said Terme of one and Twenty yeares hereby granted provided alwaies that nothing in these p'sents contained shall extend or be construed to extend to restreyne any merchants masters or others from sending any letters or pacquetts to or from the said Plantations or Colonys or any of them by any masters of Ships or other vessells or by any other person or persons which such merchants masters or others will specially imploy or intrust for the carriage of the same according to their respective direc?c?ons And the said Thomas Neale Doth for himselfe his executors administrators and assignes covenant promise and grant to and with us our heires and successors by these presents that he the said Thomas Neale his executors administrators or assignes or such person or persons as he or they shall nominate as aforesaid shall and will from time to time upon his or their receipt or receipts of any letters or Pacquetts which shall be directed into the said Iselands Colonyes and Plantations or any of them from England or any other parts or from any parts or places within the said Iselands Colonyes or Plantations to any other parts or places within the same cause the said letters or Pacquetts to be forthwith dispersed carried and delivered in the severall parts of the said Iselands Colonies and Plantations as they shall be directed and from time to time as he they or any of them shall collect or receive any letters or Pacquetts to be sent from the said Plantations Islands or Colonyes or any of them for England shall dispatch and send away the same by the first Ship that shall be bound for any Port of England to be there delivered to the next Deputy Postmaster as aforesaid and where any letters or Pacquetts shall be directed from any of the said Colonies Islands or Plantations to some other of them that he or they shall dispatch and send away the same according to the respective direc?c?ons by the first conveniency of carriage or conveyance thereof and that these services shall be performed with care and without any neglect or delay at the rates before mentioned And the said Thomas Neale doth further for himselfe his executors administrators and assignes covenant promise and grant to and with us our heires and successors by these presents That he the said Thomas Neale his executors administrators or assignes shall and will at his and their own costs and charges keep accounts in bookes fairely written of all the sum?es of money and profitts whatsoever ariseing in every yeare by the Office imployment or businesse aforesaid and of all charges thereupon and shall suffer the said Bookes to be inspected from time to time and coppies thereof or notes out of the same to be taken by such person or persons as the Com?issioners of the Treasury or High Treasurer of England for the time being shall appoint and shall and will within the Twentieth yeare of the said Terme of twenty one yeares hereby granted produce the said Bookes themselves or soe many of them as shall be then made to the Com?issioners of the Treasury or High Treasurer of England then being To the end he or they may have certaine knowledge of the yearly value of the said Office or Offices for the future benefitt of us our heires and successors And further that such publique orders as the Governors of the said respective Plantacons Islands or Colonies from time to time shall issue out for the Im?ediate service of us our heires and successors shall be dispatcht and distributed by the said respective Offices without any charge Provided that noe person or persons whatsoever shall be capable of exerciseing the said Office or Offices or any of them or any Deputac?on relateing thereunto untill he or they doe first take the oathes appointed by the Act of Parliament made in the first yeare of our reigne Entituled (An Act for the abrogateing the Oathes of Supremacy and allegiance and appointing other oathes) Provided alsoe that if it shall at any time hereafter be made appeare to us our heires or successors that this our grant is inconvenient to our subjects in generall or that the powers hereby granted or mentioned to be granted or mentioned to be granted or any of them is or are abused That then it shall and may be lawfull to and for us our heires and successors by any order of or made in our or their Privy Councill to revoake determine and make void these our Letters Patents and every clause power and thing therein contained any thing to the contrary thereof in any wise notwithstanding Provided further that if the said Thomas Neale his executors administrators or assignes shall not within the space of two yeares next after the date of these our Letters Patents establish the Post or Office thereby intended within the Colonys Islands and Plantations aforesaid according to the true intent and meaning of these Presents Then this our grant and every power matter and thing therein contained shall cease and be void any thing to the contrary thereof in any wise notwithstanding And the said Thomas Neale doth for himselfe his executors administrators and assignes covenant promise and grant to and with us our heires and successors that all letters or Pacquetts collected or received in any of the Plantations Iselands or Colonys aforesaid to be sent for England shall from time to time be carefully put up and dispatched away by the first Ship bound for any Port of England to be delivered by the next Deputy Postmaster in England without any charge to the Post Office here excepting and reserveing unto us our heires and successors the English Inland Postage of all such letters and Pacquetts last mentioned to be sent for England It being hereby intended and declared that the same shall not be accounted for to the said Thomas Neale his executors administrators or assignes but that he and they shall and is and are hereby obliged to satisfie and pay the masters of such vessells for such conveyance and delivery of such letters and pacquetts as shall be sent for

England as aforesaid and alsoe that he the said Thomas Neale his executors administrator or assignes shall and will at his and their owne proper costs and charges nominate and appoint a sufficient Officer in our City of London to receive and collect from time to time all letters and Pacquetts for any of our Colonys or Plantations aforesaid and to take care to send them duely away from time to time by the first vessell bound for any of those Parts And further that all letters com?only called State letters which are usually carried Postage free here in England shall pass free thorow all our Plantations and Iselands aforesaid And further alsoe that he the said Thomas Neale his executors administrators or assignes shall and will at the end of the first three yeares next ensueing after the date of these Presents transmitt or cause to be transmitted to the Com?issioners of the Treasury or High Treasurer of England for the time being a true and faithfull account in writeing upon oath of the whole profitts and advantage ariseing or accrewing by and the charge of settling and mannageing the said Office or Offices herein before granted or mentioned to be granted and established and shall and will alsoe keep true and faithful accounts in writeing of all the receipts and charges aforesaid relating to the said Office or Employment and that from and after the expirac?on of the said Three yeares next ensueing after the date of this our Grant the like account shall be yearly transmitted as aforesaid if thereunto required And for the better excution of the powers and direc?c?ons herein contained Wee have given and granted and by these Presents for us our heires and successors doe give and grant unto the said Thomas Neale his executors administrators and assignes full power and authority from time to time dureing the said Terme of twenty one yeares to sett up make use and have Ferrys over any River or Lake in our said Colonies Iselands or Plantations where noe Ferrys are yet made nor any grant thereof made or given to any other person or persons by us or any of our Predecessors for the better conveyance of Postage and Passengers as need shall require and to receive and take the Profitts and advantage comeing or ariseing by such Ferrys to the use and benefitt of him the said Thomas Neale his executors administrators and assignes provided always and our will and pleasure is and Wee do here for us our heires and successors Declare that in all cases where such Ferry or Ferrys are to be sett up and made over other Persons land or water the Proprietor or Proprietors thereof shall be first agreed with and his and their consent gained therein according to Law and Justice In Witnesse &c Witnesse ourselves at Westm? the seaventeenth day of February

By Writt of Privy Seale.

I certify that the foregoing is a true and authentic copy:—

R. DOUGLAS TRIMMER

Assistant Keeper of the Public Records

1 February 1894

NOTES

1. *Mass. Historical Collections*, 4th Series, Vol. VII., p. 128.
2. *Mass. Historical Collections*, 4th Series, Vol. VI., pp. 242, 256, 276.
3. Mass. Historical Collections, *4th Series, Vol. VII.*
4. Mass. Colonial Records, *I., p. 281*. Mass. Historical Collections, *3d Series, Vol. VII., p. 48.*
5. Laws and Ordinances of New Netherlands.
6. Laws and Ordinances of New Netherlands, pp. 379, 380.
7. Brodhead, *History of the State of New York*, Vol. II., pp. 196-98.
8. *Memorial History of N. Y.*, Vol. I., pp. 355-56.
9. Brodhead, *History of N. Y.*, Vol. II., p. 413.
10. *Mass. Historical Collections*, 3d Series, Vol. VII., p. 49.
11. *Mass. Historical Collections*, 3d Series, Vol. VII., p. 48.
12. *Mass. Records*, Vol. V., pp. 147, 148.
13. Colonial Records of Connecticut, *Vol. II., p. 242.*
14. Brodhead, Vol. I.
15. *Colonial Documents of N. Y.*, Vol. III., pp. 349-350.
16. Colonial Documents of N. Y., *Vol. III., p. 355.*
17. Colonial Documents of N. Y., *Vol. III.*
18. *Connecticut Records*, Vol. III., pp. 392, 393, 398.
19. Letter Book of Sam. Sewall, *Vol. I., p. 25.*
20. The discrepancy in dates leads to the supposition that John Perry served as bearer before his actual appointment.

21. Colonial Documents of N. Y., *Vol. III., p. 682.*
22. Mass. Provincial Records.
23. *Mass. Historical Collections*, 3d series, Vol VII., pp. 50-51.
24. *Mass. Historical Collections*, 3d series, Vol. VII., p. 51, also Palfrey's *History of New England.*
25. Palfrey, IV., p. 329.
26. Colonial Documents of N. Y., *Vol. IV, p. 200.*
27. Journal of the Legislative Council of New York, *Vol. I, pp. 26, 31, 32, 34.*
28. Journal of the Assembly, *pp. 26, 28.*
29. Copied from the original MS. at Albany.
30. Journal of Legislative Council, *I., pp. 79, 80.*
31. Journal of the Assembly.
32. *Journal of the Legislative Council*, I., pp. 136, 137, 138, 143.
33. Journal Legislative Council, *I., 186, 187, 189.*
34. *Journal of the Assembly*, pp. 154, 226, 227, 234.
35. *Journal of the Assembly*, pp. 198, 200, 203.
36. Colonial Documents of N. Y., *IV., pp. 1167-68.*
37. Journal of the Council, *I., p. 247.*
38. Journal of the Assembly, *219, 223, 224.*
39. Journal of the Legislative Council, *I., p. 285.*
40. Colonial Documents of N. Y., *IV., p. 317.*
41. Colonial Documents of N. Y., *IV., p. 1017.*
42. Colonial Documents of N. Y., *Vol. IV., p. 1113.*
43. Colonial Documents, *p. 1120.*
44. Mass. Historical Collections, *3d Series, Vol. VII.*
45. *Mass. Historical Collections*, 3d Series, Vol. VII., pp. 55-60.

46. The successor of Duncan and famous as the publisher of the *News Letter.*
47. *Mass. Historical Collections*, 3d Series, Vol. VII., pp. 60, 69.
48. *Mass. Historical Collections*, 3d Series, Vol. VII., pp. 56-60.
49. *Mass. Historical Collections*, 3d Series, Vol. VII., p. 80.
50. *N. H. Provincial Papers*, Vol. II., p. 100.
51. *N. H. Provincial Papers*, Vol. II., p. 101.
52. *N. H. Provincial Papers*, Vol. III., p. 11.
53. Copied from the original, also in *Hist. Magazine*, Vol. III., p. 351.
54. *N. H. Provincial Papers*, Vol. III., p. 18.
55. *N. H. Provincial Papers*, Vol. III., p. 30.
56. *N. H. Provincial Papers*, Vol. III., pp. 61, 248, 257, 279.
57. *N. H. Provincial Papers*, Vol. III., p. 304.
58. *N. H. Provincial Papers*, Vol. III., p. 343.
59. Colonial Records of Rhode Island.
60. Colonial Records of Connecticut, *Vol. IV., p. 123.*
61. *Colonial Records*, Vol. IV., p. 246-47.
62. *Colonial Records*, Vol. IV., p. 468.
63. Watson, Vol. II., p. 391. Winsor, *Narrative and Critical History*, Vol. III., p. 491. *Historical Magazine*, Vol. III., p. 221.
64. *Historical Magazine*, Vol. III., p. 223.
65. Penn and Logan Correspondence.
66. Duke of Yorke's Laws, *p. 224.*
67. Pennsylvania Colonial Records, *Vol. I., p. 524.*
68. Duke of Yorke's Laws, *p. 262.*
69. *Martin's* Bench and Bar of Philadelphia, *pp. 126-130.*

70. *Pennsylvania Magazine*, Vol. IX., p. 444.

71. Copied from the original.

72. *Pennsylvania Magazine*, Vol. IX., p. 444.

73. Hening's *Statutes at Large*, Vol. II., p. 109.

74. Hening's *Statutes at Large*, Vol. III., pp. 112, 115.

75. Cooper's *Statutes at Large*, Vol. II., pp. 188-89.

76. Cooper's *Statutes at Large*, Vol. II, p. 308.

77. *Iredell,* Laws of North Carolina.

78. *Mass. Historical Collections*, 6th Series, Vol. V., pp. 64, 65, 66, 70.

79. Penn and Logan Correspondence*, Vol. II., p. 257.*

80. *Mass. Historical Collections*, 6th Series, Vol. V., pp. 52, 101, 116, 140.